This *Peppa Pig* book
belongs to

WITHDRAWN FROM STOCK

....

LADYBIRD BOOKS

UK | USA | Canada | Ireland | Australia | India | New Zealand | South Africa

Ladybird Books is part of the Penguin Random House group of companies whose addresses can be found at global.penguinrandomhouse.com.

www.penguin.co.uk   www.puffin.co.uk   www.ladybird.co.uk

Penguin
Random House
UK

First published 2022
001

Licensed by

Printed in China

The authorized representative in the EEA is Penguin Random House Ireland, Morrison Chambers, 32 Nassau Street, Dublin D02 YH68

A CIP catalogue record for this book is available from the British Library

ISBN: 978-0-241-54350-4

All correspondence to:
Ladybird Books, Penguin Random House Children's
One Embassy Gardens, 8 Viaduct Gardens, London SW11 7BW

Note for Adults

Some of the activities in this book are "make-and-do" craft activities, and all these craft activities require adult help. Those that need particularly close supervision have been given the following icon:

No matter the age or ability of a child, always do yourself any steps that involve the use of an oven, scissors, knives or very strong glue.

Contents

Christmas Carousel 6
Craft Time: Snow Much Fun! 7
Christmas Costumes 8
Let's Dance! 9
Delivering Presents 11
Story Time: Molly Mole 12
Buried Treasure 18
Fluttery Butterfly Wings................... 19
Very Important Jobs 20
Cool Science 22
Peppa's Clubhouse 23
Story Time: Playgroup Star 24
Perfect Picture 30
Whose Painting? 31
Woodland Club 32
A Very Big Ice Cream! 34

Counting Quiz 35
Craft Time: Peppa's House 36
Odd One Out 38
Bug Hotel 39
Roman Day 40
Chocolate-Puddle Biscuits 43
Marble-Run Fun! 44
Story Time: Sailing Boat 46
Story Quiz 52
Craft Time: Paper Boat 53
Go! Go! Go! Game 54
Peppa Loves Yoga 56
Sunshine Shadows 57
Which Season? 58
Bubbles, Bubbles Everywhere! 60
Mountain Climbing 61

Christmas Carousel

Wheeeeee! Peppa, George and Suzy Sheep are at a magical Christmas fair! Join the dots and colour in the picture to find out what they are doing.

How many red-nosed reindeer can you spot in the picture?

Craft Time: Snow Much Fun!

These pretty decorations are easy to make.

You will need:
* A square sheet of white paper
* Scissors
* Pencil
* White thread
* Sticky tape

Every snowflake that falls is unique, which means they all look completely different!

1 Fold a sheet of paper in half, and then in half again to make a smaller square.

2 On the open side, cut a curve from one corner to the other so that, if you opened the paper out, you would have a rough circle.

3 Keeping the paper folded, draw some random shapes on one side, and then cut them out.

4 Unfold the paper to reveal your pretty snowflake.

5 Tape a piece of white thread to the top of your snowflake and hang it in the room or on your Christmas tree.

WITHDRAWN FROM STOCK

Christmas Costumes

It's time for the playgroup Christmas party. Peppa and George can't decide what to wear, so they're holding a festive fashion show!

Can you work out who comes next in each row?

1  ?
___

2  ?
___

3  ?
___

4  ?
___

Answers: 1. Peppa, 2. George, 3. Peppa, 4. Peppa

Delivering Presents

Ho! Ho! Ho! Peppa, George and Daddy Pig
are delivering Christmas presents to everyone.
Do they have all the gifts on their list?

Mummy Pig

Granny Pig

Grandpa Pig

Madame Gazelle

Miss Rabbit

Colour in a Christmas decoration for each present you spot.

"Do you mean like this?" asks Molly. She digs a hole in the ground.
DRRRRRILLL!
"Wow!" say Peppa and Rebecca.
Molly disappears down into the hole . . .

Pop! Molly pops her head up on the other side of the sandpit.
"You're amazing at digging, Molly," says Peppa.
"I'm a mole," replies Molly. "Moles are *very* good diggers."
Peppa, Rebecca and Molly laugh.

The bell rings, and it's time to go home.
Mummy Rabbit comes to collect Rebecca. Then Molly's mummy arrives.
"Can my new friend Peppa come to our house to play?" asks Molly.
"If it's OK with her daddy," says Mummy Mole.
"Of course," says Daddy Pig. "I'll pick you up later, Peppa."

Peppa rides in Molly's car to her house. She is very excited, and so is Molly.
They giggle *all* the way. "Hee! Hee! Hee!"

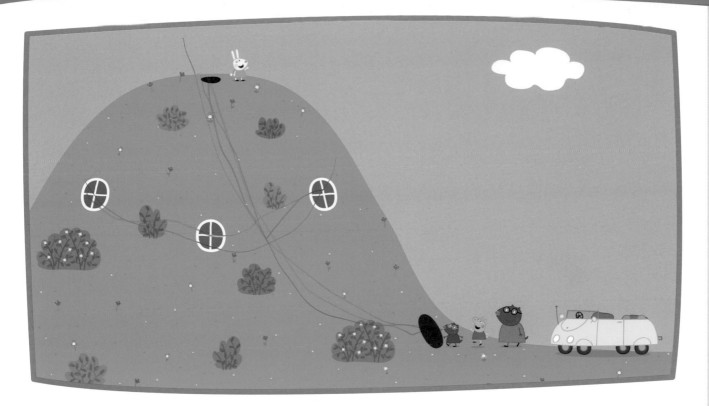

"This is my house!" says Molly when they arrive at a hill.
Peppa is confused. "But this is Rebecca's house," she says.
"Hello," says Rebecca, waving from the top of the hill.
"We've moved in *underneath* Rebecca's house," explains Molly.

Molly and Mummy Mole take Peppa through a little round hole at the
bottom of the hill. Molly and her family live deep underground.
"The house isn't finished yet," says Molly. "My mummy and daddy are
still building it."

Daddy Mole is in Molly's room when they arrive.
"This is my new friend Peppa," says Molly.
"Hello!" says Peppa.
"Delighted to meet you," he replies.

After a while, Daddy Pig arrives to pick up Peppa.
"Come inside," says Mummy Mole. "Excuse the mess . . . we're building an extension."
"It takes lots of people to build an extension," says Daddy Pig.
"Actually, Daddy Mole and I are just building it ourselves," says Mummy Mole.

"The good thing about digging your own house is that you do what you want, where you want," says Daddy Mole. "You can even put a door here."
Daddy Mole digs a hole in the ceiling and pops his head up through it.
"Oh, hello," says Daddy Rabbit. "A doorway in the floor, what a good idea!"

Daddy Mole climbs back down his ladder.
"It's great having a hole between our houses," says Rebecca. "Now you can come and play with me any time you want, Molly!"
"And you can come and play with me any time you want!" says Molly.
Molly and Rebecca love being neighbours!

Buried Treasure

Molly is very good at digging. Can you help Molly and her friends find their way through this underground maze to the treasure?

Fluttery Butterfly Wings

Flutter, flutter! Gerald Giraffe has made some beautiful butterfly wings. Use your favourite pencils or crayons to colour them in.

Draw some butterflies fluttering around!

Very Important Jobs

Peppa is at playgroup, learning all about different jobs. Do you know where everyone works? Draw lines to match them to the right places.

20

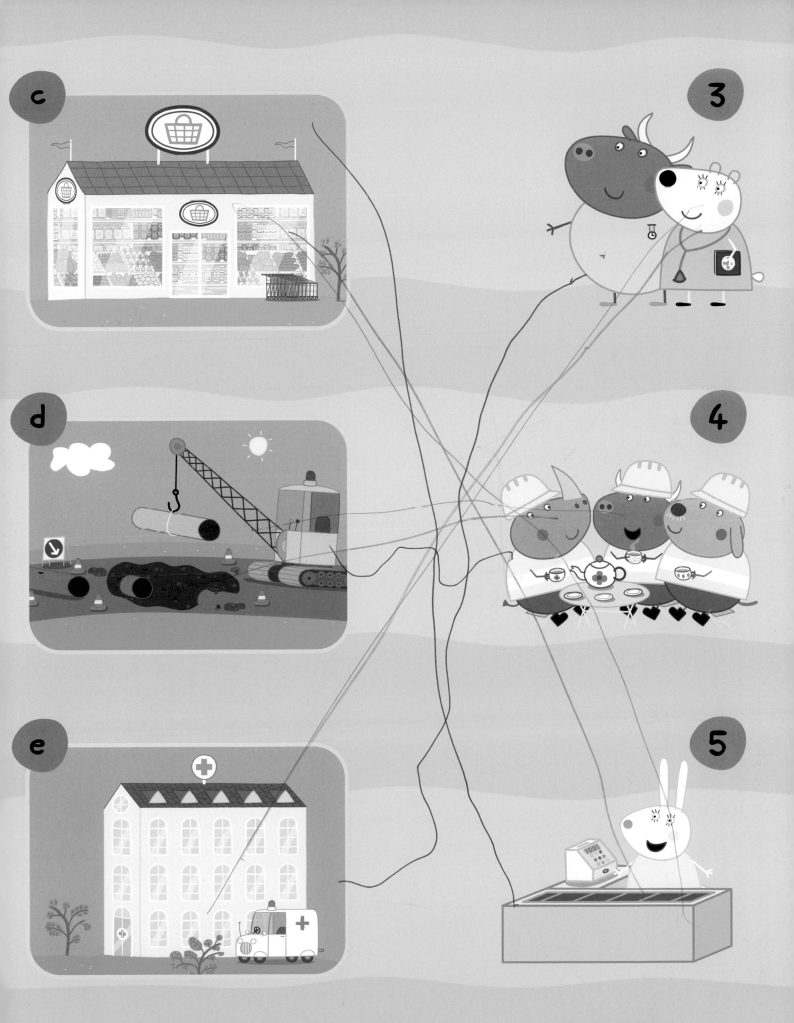

Answers: a–2, b–1, c–5, d–4, e–3

Cool Science

Peppa and Mandy Mouse are looking at different things through a microscope. Microscopes make things appear bigger! What are they looking at? Match the close-ups to the objects.

Answers: a-4, b-2, c-1, d-3

Peppa's Clubhouse

Peppa and her friends have their own special clubhouse to play in! Use the numbers to help you colour the picture, and then decorate it for them.

Story Time
Playgroup Star

Peppa and George are painting pictures at playgroup.
"I *love* painting pictures," says Peppa. "Do you like painting, George?"
George giggles. "Hee! Hee!" He loves painting pictures, too.

Peppa shows Madame Gazelle her painting. "It's me and my family."
"Where are you all?" asks Madame Gazelle.
"*Inside* the house," explains Peppa.
"Of course," says Madame Gazelle. "What a wonderful picture.
You've earned a playgroup star!"
"WOW!" cries Peppa. "Thank you, Madame Gazelle."

When Mummy and Daddy Pig arrive, Peppa shows them her painting.
"Mummy! Daddy! Look!" she cries. "I got a playgroup star!"
"That's fantastic, Peppa," says Daddy Pig. "Well done."

"Did *you* get lots of playgroup stars when *you* were little, Mummy?" asks Peppa.
"Oh yes," says Mummy Pig.
"Daddy," says Peppa, "did you get lots of playgroup stars, too?"
"Er," says Daddy Pig. "I can't remember."
"I'm pretty sure you didn't get one. Did you?" says Mummy Pig.

A long time ago when Mummy and Daddy Pig were little, Madame Gazelle was their teacher. Mummy and Daddy Pig loved painting at playgroup – just like Peppa and George!

One day, Madame Gazelle gave Mummy Pig a playgroup star for her painting . . . but Daddy Pig didn't get one.

"Are you sad that you never got a playgroup star, Daddy?" asks Peppa.

"Well, I have done other things in my life to be proud of," says Daddy Pig.

"And it was a long time ago."

That night, Daddy Pig goes up into the loft to look for his
favourite playgroup picture to show Peppa and George.
"I know it's up here somewhere," he tells them.

"Ah, here's my old school bag," says Daddy Pig. "And here is
my favourite picture from playgroup."
"WOW!" cries Peppa. "It's a very good dragon, Daddy!"
"*Grrr!*" growls George.
"It's sad it didn't get a playgroup star, Daddy," says Peppa.

The next day, Peppa takes Daddy Pig's picture to playgroup.

"It's not fair, Peppa," says Suzy Sheep. "You're too good at painting."

"It's not my painting," says Peppa. "It's my daddy's."

"Oh, not so good for a grown-up," says Suzy.

"He drew it a long time ago when he was little," explains Peppa.

"Peppa, have you done another wonderful picture?" asks Madame Gazelle.

"No," says Peppa. "This is my daddy's."

"Ah, yes," says Madame Gazelle. "I remember your daddy did like to paint."

"But you never gave him a playgroup star," says Peppa.

"Didn't I?" asks Madame Gazelle. "Well, I must give him one for *this*."
Daddy Pig comes over, and Madame Gazelle turns around.
"Daddy Pig," says Madame Gazelle, "you deserve a playgroup star!"
She puts a big gold star on Daddy Pig's painting.

"Ho! Ho!" says Daddy Pig. "I've never been so proud."
Daddy Pig *is* a playgroup star.
"Hooray for Daddy Pig!" everyone cheers. "Ha! Ha! Ha!"

Perfect Picture

What will Peppa draw now? Can you help her make another wonderful picture? When you've finished your picture, join the dots to give yourself your very own playgroup star!

Whose Painting?

Oh dear . . . the playgroup pictures are all muddled up!
Follow the lines to find out who each picture belongs to.

31

Woodland Club

Peppa and her friends are at Woodland Club, building shelters with Mr Wolf. Look closely at the two pictures. Can you find five differences between them?

Who can you spot in the pictures? Tick the box below each friend you find.

Colour in a leaf as you spot each difference.

33

A Very Big Ice Cream!

Wow! Peppa has a GIANT ice cream! What flavours does she have? Use your pencils or crayons to colour in the picture.

What flavour ice cream is your favourite?

Counting Quiz

It's time for Mr Potato's fruit-and-vegetable quiz!
Can you help Peppa and her friends count how many
of each fruit and vegetable there are?

4 🥕 P 🥦 3 🍎 5 🍌 2 🔴

Which fruit or vegetable is there the most of?

Craft Time: Peppa's House

Build a house like Peppa's, with a red tiled roof and yellow walls.

You will need:

* Square cardboard box with flaps
* Thick card
* Masking tape
* Pencil
* Scissors
* Thin white, blue and red card
* PVA glue
* Paintbrush
* Poster or acrylic paints
* Black pipe cleaners or cocktail sticks

1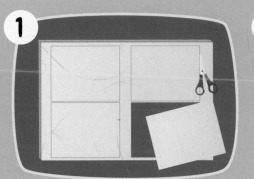

Cut four pieces of thick card into the same size and shape as the box's flaps.

2

Stick the card to the flaps. Tape the two longer flaps together to make the roof.

3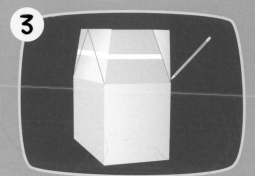

Hold the smaller flaps up and draw along the shape of the roof on each flap.

4

Fold along the pencil lines towards the roof and push the corners inside.

5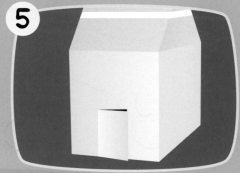

Cut out a front door, leaving one side attached, so the door can open and close.

6

Paint the house the same colours as Peppa's house, and then glue on the windows.

7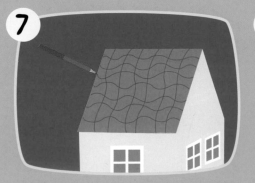

Glue sheets of red card to the sloped roof. Use red paint or a red pen to draw on the tiles.

8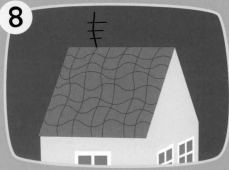

Make an aerial out of black pipe cleaners or black-painted cocktail sticks.

To make the windows:

Cut out squares of white card as shown. Cut out four squares in each to make the window frames. Glue a piece of blue card behind each window, and then stick them to the side of the house.

Your pipe-cleaner or cocktail-stick aerial can be pushed through and fixed in place with a blob of PVA glue.

Peppa and George

Make a mini Peppa and mini George to play in your house!

Templates

You will need:
* Card
* Scissors
* Paints or coloured pencils
* Craft sticks
* PVA glue

Copy or trace the templates on to card. Cut them out, colour them in, and then glue them on to craft sticks. *Snort!*

Odd One Out

Daddy Pig has asked Peppa to spot the odd one out in each group of things. Can you help her? Point to or draw a circle around each odd one out.

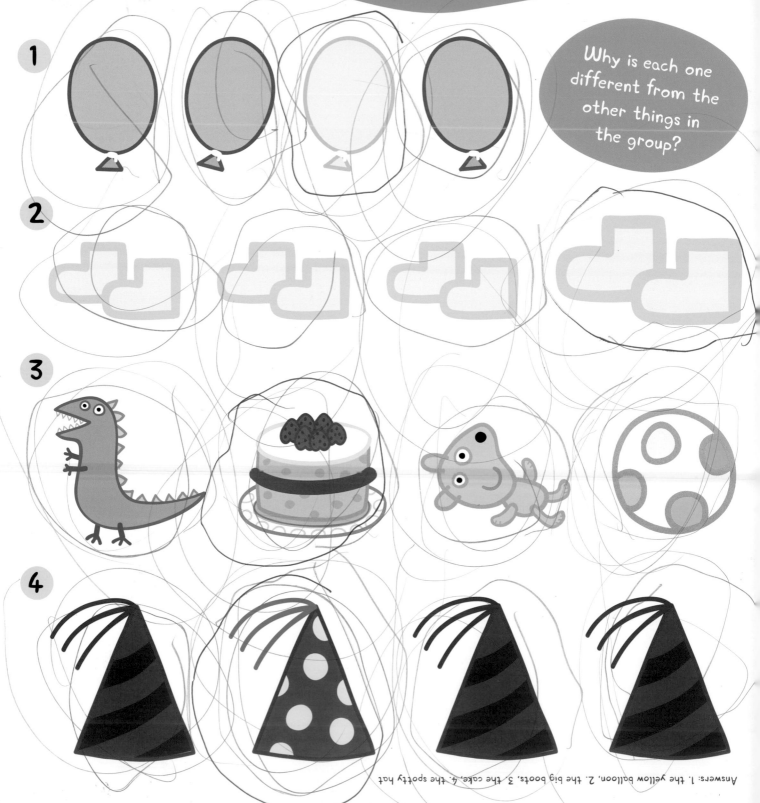

Why is each one different from the other things in the group?

38

Bug Hotel

Peppa and George are looking at all the minibeasts in and around the bug hotel. Which ones are the biggest?

Point to or draw a circle around the BIGGEST bee, ladybird, butterfly and snail.

Roman Day

Hee! Hee! Peppa and George are really enjoying
Roman Day with Granny and Grandpa Pig!

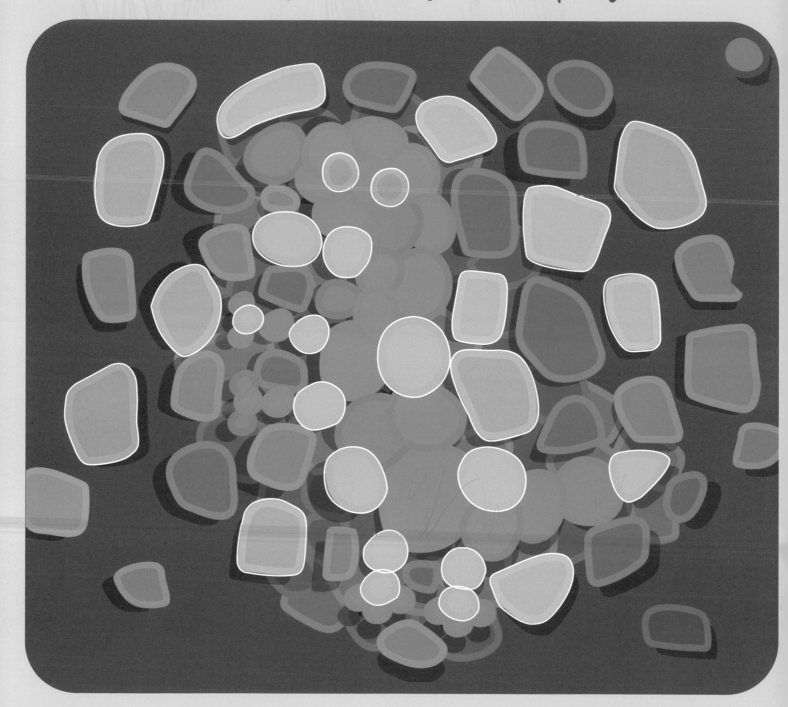

Help them make a mosaic of George's dinosaur.
A mosaic is a picture made up of different shapes.
Ask a grown-up to help cut out the coloured-paper shapes
opposite, and then stick them on to the picture.

You will need:
* Scissors
* PVA glue

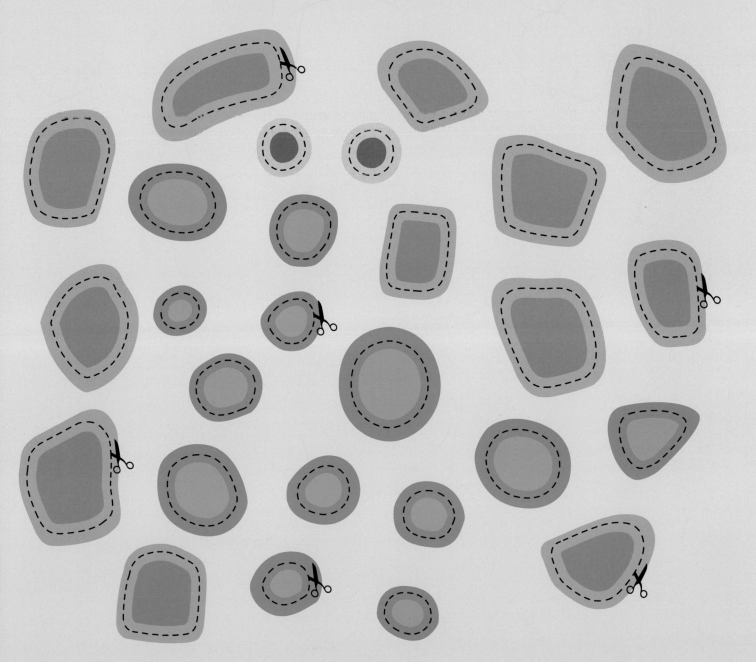

Chocolate-Puddle Biscuits

Shape these tasty boot biscuits out of cookie dough and dip them in chocolate puddles! Yum! Yum!

 Preheat the oven to 180°C (gas mark 4) and lightly grease a flat baking tray.

 Mix together the butter and sugar, mix in the egg yolks, and then stir in the flour.

3 Add just enough milk to bring the mixture together into a soft dough.

4 Sprinkle some flour on to a work surface. Divide the ball of dough into three pieces, divide each ball in half, then in half again, to make 12 balls.

5 Roll out each ball into a sausage shape. Turn up the bottom of each sausage and press it flat to make a boot shape.

6 Bake the biscuit boots for 10-15 minutes, until golden brown. Sprinkle with caster sugar, then leave to cool.

You will need:
* 100g butter, softened
* 100g caster sugar plus extra for sprinkling
* 2 egg yolks
* 200g plain flour, sifted
* 1-2 tablespoons milk
* Large bar of milk chocolate

Makes 12 biscuit boots

Melt a large bar of milk chocolate in a microwave or over a pan of simmering water, and then pour the chocolate into a shallow bowl.

Dip the boots in the cooled muddy chocolate puddle — and eat! *Snort!*

Marble-Run Fun!

Yippee! Daddy Pig is helping Peppa and George build a giant marble run in their bedroom! What can you spot in the picture?

Colour in a marble as you find each thing.

45

Story  Time
Sailing Boat

Grandpa Pig is taking Peppa and George sailing.
"Ahoy there, Grandpa Pig!" says Mr Stallion.
"Hello," says Grandpa Pig. "We're just going out for a sail."
"It's a bit early for sailing," says Mrs Corgi. "You can't go now."
"Thank you for your advice," says Grandpa Pig, walking to his boat.

"Grandpa," says Peppa, "your friends said that we can't go sailing."
"They don't know what they're talking about," says Grandpa Pig.
He jumps on to his boat with Peppa and George.
"Oh bother," he says, seeing that his boat is stuck in the mud.
"The tide seems to be out."

"So we *can't* go sailing, Grandpa?" asks Peppa.
"Don't worry! The water will come back again soon," says Grandpa Pig.
"Look!" cries Peppa. "The water *is* coming back!"
The water lifts Grandpa Pig's boat out of the mud.
"We're bobbing up and down!" cries Peppa.

"Let's go sailing!" shouts Grandpa Pig.
"Aye-aye, Captain Grandpa!" shouts Peppa.
"Off we go," says Grandpa Pig as he sails his boat.
Peppa and George giggle. "Hee! Hee! Hee!" Sailing is *lots* of fun.

Mr Stallion and Mrs Corgi sail up to Grandpa Pig's boat.

"Ahoy there, Grandpa Pig," calls Mrs Corgi.

"Time to head back, old chap," says Mr Stallion, "or you'll get stuck in the mud."

"Right you are, thank you," says Grandpa Pig. "Bye-eee!"

But Grandpa Pig doesn't listen to his friends. He thinks he knows more about sailing, and suddenly . . . *SPLAT!* Grandpa Pig's boat stops bobbing.

"Ah. The tide seems to have gone out," says Grandpa Pig.

"Are we stuck in the mud again, Grandpa?" asks Peppa.

"Er, yes," says Grandpa Pig. "But only until the tide changes. Then the water will lift us up again."

"When will the water come back, Grandpa?" asks Peppa.
"Er . . . tomorrow morning," says Grandpa Pig. "We'll just have
to spend the night on the boat."
"A sleepover!" cheers Peppa. "Hooray!"
Grandpa Pig calls Granny Pig to tell her they are spending the night
on the boat, and then he takes Peppa and George below deck.

"Here is where you will sleep," says Grandpa Pig, showing Peppa and George
two little beds.
"Oooooh!" cry Peppa and George.
They climb into their beds, say night-night to Grandpa Pig, and soon they fall . . .

. . . fast asleep. *Zzzzzzz!*

"Night-night, Peppa and George," says Grandpa Pig as he tucks himself into his sleeping bag under the twinkling stars. *Zzzzzzz!*

When Peppa and George wake up the next morning, they can feel the boat bobbing up and down again.

"We're bobbing up and down!" cries Peppa.

"Time to sail home!" says Grandpa Pig.

"Aye-aye, Captain Grandpa," says Peppa.

Grandpa Pig sails his boat home.

Granny Pig is waiting. "Hello, my little ones," she says. "Did you have a nice time?"

"Yes!" cries Peppa. "We got stuck in the mud and had a sleepover!"

Granny Pig chuckles.

Peppa loves sailing. *Everyone* loves sailing!

Story Quiz

How much do you remember about Peppa's sailing boat story? Try answering these questions to find out.

1. What did Peppa go sailing in? Draw a circle around the right vehicle.

a

b

c

2. Who did Peppa go sailing with? Colour in everyone she sailed with.

a

b

c

3. Where did they sleep? Colour in the circle next to the right place.

a

b

c

4. Who came to meet them when they'd finished sailing? Draw a tick next to your answer.

a

b

c

Craft Time: Paper Boat

Make a paper boat from a sheet of A4 paper!

1

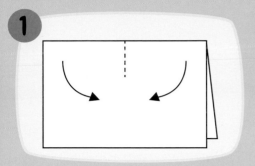

Fold the paper in half, and then make a crease in the centre, at the top.

2

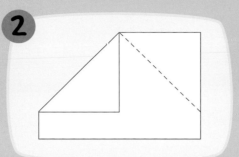

Fold down each corner towards the middle.

3

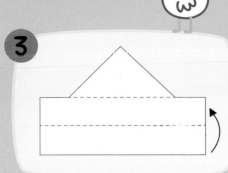

Fold the edges of the paper up on both sides, then open out the paper in a hat shape.

4

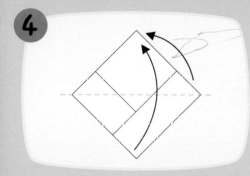

Bring the corners of the hat towards each other and flatten the shape into a square.

5

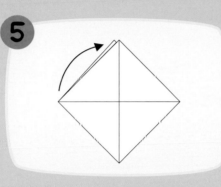

Hold the open corners of the square and fold each one up to make flattened triangles, as shown in the drawing in step 6.

6

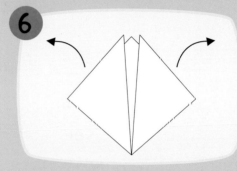

Flatten the triangle into a square by opening it up in the middle to fold the two bottom corners together and fold flat into a square.

7

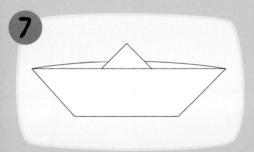

Gently pull the sides of the triangle out to make a boat shape.

Make Up a Pirate Story

Shiver me timbers! Captain George and Pirate Peppa have followed a treasure map all the way to a desert island. They start to dig in the sand for buried treasure when suddenly some more pirates arrive . . . Make up a story about what happens next.

Go! Go! Go! Game

It's a very busy day, and Peppa and her friends are on the go! Play this game to see who can make it home first.

How to play:

1. Use counters (you could use balls of screwed-up scrap paper!) for each player, and place them on "Let's go!".

2. Take it in turns to roll a dice and move around the board, following the directions as you go. If you land on a vehicle, look at the box below to see what you should do.

3. The first player to reach the finish is the winner!

Move on 2 spaces.

Camper van: Cruise in the camper van!

Whizz along 3 spaces.

Miss Rabbit's helicopter: Miss Rabbit picks you up in her helicopter!

Zoom along 1 space.

Playgroup bus: Hooray! The playgroup bus is on its way

Drive on 1 space.

Peppa's family car: Brrmm, Brrmm! Time to get in the car.

Sail on 1 space.

Captain Dog's boat: Ahoy there! Hop aboard Captain Dog's boat.

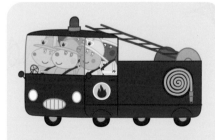

Speed along 2 spaces.

Fire engine: Nee-naa! The firefighters give you a lift!

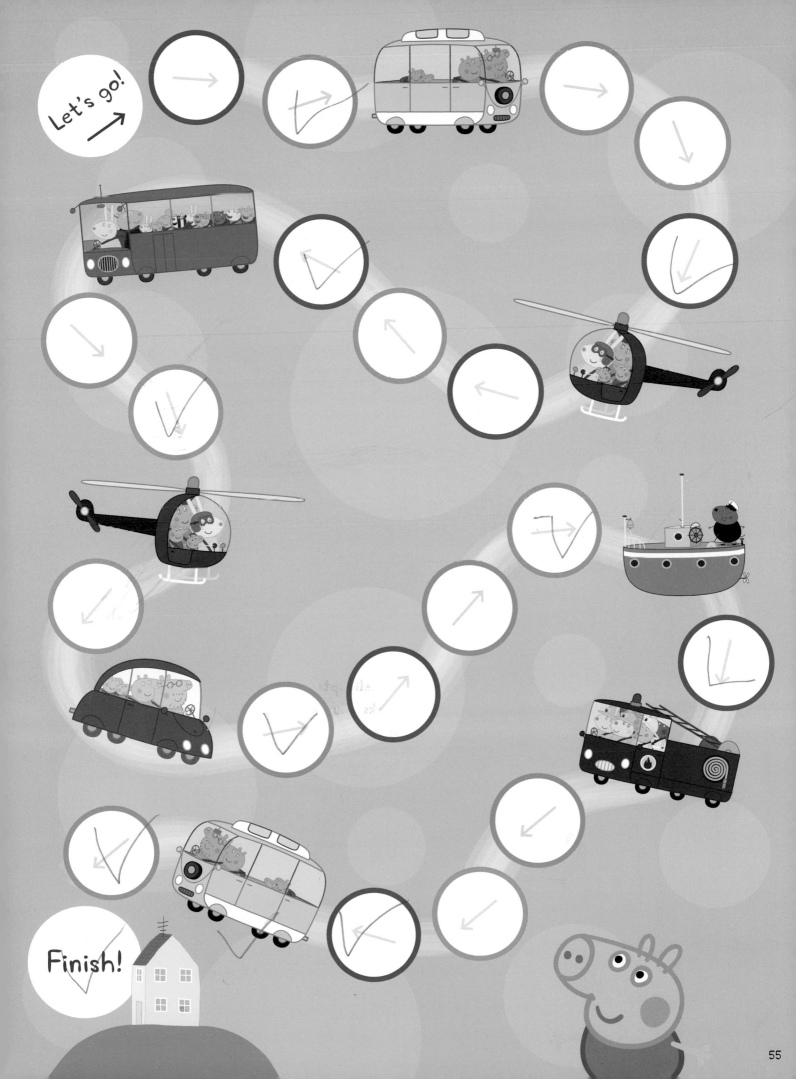

Let's go!

Finish!

55

Peppa Loves Yoga

And breathe . . . Peppa and her friends love yoga.
Take a deep breath in and out, and relax while you
colour in this peaceful picture.

Sunshine Shadows

It's a lovely sunny day, and the children are looking at their shadows. Can you draw lines to match everyone to the right shadow shapes?

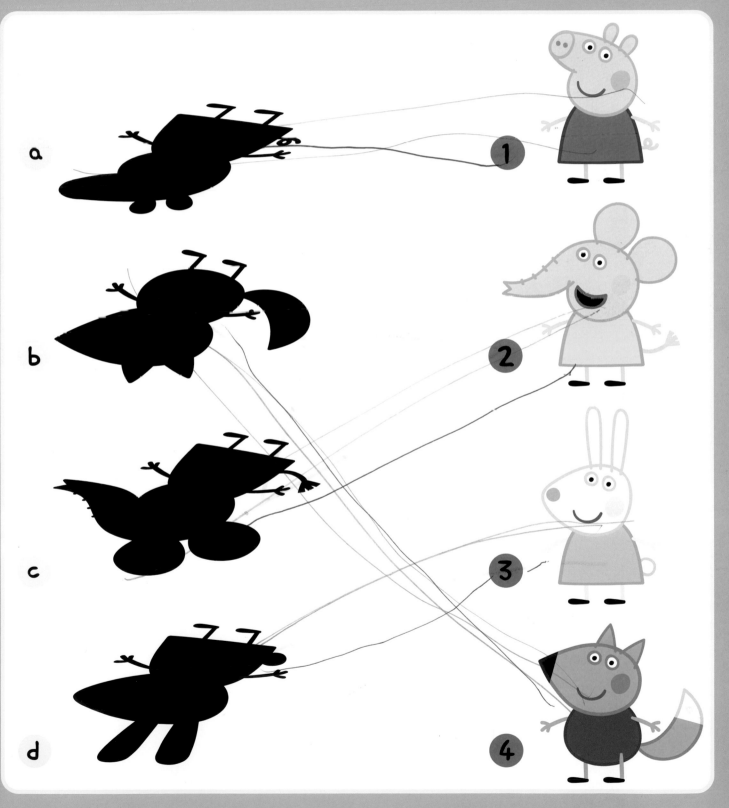

Answers: a-1, b-4, c-2, d-3

Which Season?

Peppa loves seeing how the apple tree changes each season.
Do you know which season each picture is showing?
Trace over the dotted lines to find out.

spring

summer

Which season is your favourite?

autumn

winter

59

Bubbles, Bubbles Everywhere!

Pffft! Peppa is blowing bubbles! But where have they all gone? Fill the page with as many bubbles as you can. They can be big ones or little ones . . . and even different shapes!

Mountain Climbing

Peppa and George love going to the climbing centre!
Help them reach the top of the mountain by drawing a way
from the start to the finish using only the green holds.

When you reach the finish, draw a flag on the top, and then wave to everyone down below!

Finish

Start

Look out for these other great *Peppa Pig* books!

Sticker activity books

Board books

Lift-the-flap books

Picture books